The Lancelot Closes at Five

The Lancelot Closes at Five

by MARJORIE WIENMAN SHARMAT

Inside illustrations by Lisl Weil

Cover illustration by Daryl Cagle

SCHOLASTIC BOOK SERVICES
New York Toronto London Auckland Sydney Tokyo

0-590-32018-1

12 11 10 9 8 7 6 5 4 3 2 1   10   1 2 3 4 5 6/8

Printed in the U. S. A.   11

for my husband, Mitch,
who has read, analyzed,
perceived, suggested,
and helped in so many ways
with all my books

Chapter
1

The map-makers are just getting around to discovering Camelot. My parents discovered it much sooner.

When they found Camelot it consisted of three model homes, the Excalibur, the Lancelot and the Guinevere, and a brochure. The brochure said that Camelot would become "a community of distinguished residences built on twenty-one beautiful tree-shaded acres of land in Shady Landing, New York." Each model home and the village of Shady Landing were described in language that I would not be caught dead using. Words like "exquisite," "gracious" and "elegant." But there were other words like "trees," "convenient to schools," "uncrowded classes" and "clean air" that really got to me. I couldn't truthfully use any of these words to describe what it was like living in our five-room apartment in Brooklyn.

We decided to settle in Camelot because of three other words spoken by my father: "Sound investment value." My parents picked the Excalibur because it had one more bathroom than the others. We had to wait eight months while our house was being built. The builders had promised that it would be ready in four months.

"Eight months is excellent," said my father. "That's only double the promised time. I had expected to be lied to upward of ten months."

It wasn't easy for us to leave Brooklyn. Us being me, Abby, my older sister Laurie, commonly known as a teenager, my ten-year-old brother Clyde, occasionally known as a nuisance, and my parents.

In Brooklyn I had at least six close friends and a neighborhood I was used to. Before I left, when I had to write an essay in school, I called mine "Leaving a Place Forever." My teacher said it was written "with sensitivity" and was "well thought out." I hope she didn't think my father helped me do the thinking. My father is a professional writer. Which has something to do with how

t to Camelot. Or I should say how we could *afford*
there.

father has written about two dozen mystery books.
ther says it's because he writes fast and he writes
t we've been eating regularly. His latest book is
ave the Key in the Mailbox. It sold around
pies in the hardcover edition. Then it went into
with a new picture on the cover. It sold
pies, including 189 to a bunch of lonely sol-
diers stationed in the Aleutian Islands. It made enough
money so that we could think about moving to a place
like Camelot. But why did the paperback sell so well?

"It was *not* because of the half-naked woman on the cover," my mother kept saying over and over to my father. "They bought your *words*. They bought your paperback words because they cost less than your hardcover words."

Clyde said, "I liked the key and the mailbox picture on the first cover because it was what the story inside was about. I'm going to be a writer when I grow up, and I'm going to make the picture on the outside look just like what's going on inside."

Laurie and I tried not to get into these discussions because we didn't want to upset our father. We both agreed that the half-naked woman was the reason the book sold so well. But we hoped our mother could convince our father that it wasn't so. There were long family talks about morality and dirty money, but in the end, in Laurie's and my opinions it was due solely to the naked lady's financial assistance that we moved to Camelot.

It rained the day we moved. And our new basement was a new flooded basement. There were other surprises, too. The stove didn't work, doorknobs came off, and three windows seemed to be nailed to their sills.

We had plenty of company for weeks—repairmen. My mother thought of repairmen as supermen. They knew things she never would know. Never. Not if she studied repair manuals till she was eighty and took courses on

the side. The repairmen were Authority and she was Ignorance. And in every encounter with them, the score
was always Authority 100: Ignorance 0. The men would
come into the house and fix whatever they wanted and

tell her whatever they wanted, and all she ever said was
O.K. My father knew slightly less than my mother about
repairs.

Somehow most of our problems got taken care of except for the floods. My father sent a complaining letter to
Lucar Properties, the builders. He received a letter back
saying that they had received his letter. Finally they sent
some men over who looked at our basement, shook their
heads, and left. From time to time they sent other men
over. They too looked at our basement, shook their
heads, and left.

Our house was known officially in the village records as Sheet 10, Block 258, Lot 4. To me that was a better name than the Excalibur. We also got a plain street name, Oakdale Road. But the village people still referred to us and our neighbors as the Camelot People. So far, there were only ten houses built and occupied, but they were already blaming the Camelot People for tearing up their beautiful old trees to build houses. The Camelot People were this. The Camelot People were that. Camelot sounded like a fungus disease that was contaminating twenty-one acres of Shady Landing.

But we didn't mind. My father said that the village would get used to us, and when we started to pay our taxes, they might even learn to love us.

Immediately I got myself a friend, Heather "call me Hutch" Hutchins. Hutch's family built a Lancelot two doors down from us, and in addition, Hutch and I got put in some of the same classes at school. I liked Hutch from the beginning because she always wanted to be with me, and that made me feel like I was great to be with. I also liked Hutch for the very practical reason that she lived in Camelot. In Brooklyn I was part of the scene, but in Shady Landing I was new and I stuck out, me and the other Camelot kids. I didn't like to stick out. At least with Hutch, I had somebody to stick out with. Hutch would have been noticed anywhere. I met her at school, not at Camelot. I hadn't seen her when she moved in two days before. Anyway she's more noticeable when she's heard than when she's seen. I first heard her in Miss Forbes's Social Studies class. The class was having a discussion about England in the second half of the nineteenth century and, as Miss Forbes put it, "the forces that helped shape it." When she asked for the names of "outstanding personalities" of the period, Monroe Firestone, who liked to fool around, offered Jack the Ripper. Everybody laughed but Miss Forbes. She liked to "encourage lively discussions" and she said that, in his own way, he *was* a prominent personality. She said that his true identity was still a mystery but "we suspect that he might have been a member of royalty, possibly a relative of Queen Victoria."

Monroe said, "Royalty or not, boy was he sick!"

At this point, Hutch came into the discussion. She said very simply, "I believe that Jack the Ripper ate the wrong foods. Most likely he ate too much protein. That would do it."

"Do what?" asked Miss Forbes.

"Make him the way he was," said Hutch. "Then again, maybe it was too many additives, too many artificials. I bet that along with his knife, he carried around a lot of little bottles with pills. Someone should have helped a person like that. Helped him to be a natural person again. That's the key word. Natural."

After that nobody knew what to say. The class was stunned.

Finally Miss Forbes said, "I think you are confusing the problems of today with the problems of yesterday. But at any rate, I do not believe that eating right would have changed what was wrong with Jack the Ripper."

Hutch glared at Miss Forbes. Obviously she was a Non-Believer, an atheist who did not worship the Natural Foods God.

Miss Forbes changed the subject to Disraeli.

After class I went over to Hutch and said, "My father is intrigued by Jack the Ripper. He might like to hear your theory."

And that's how we became friends.

Laurie also got herself a friend, Jill. And she flipped over a few boys, but mostly a senior named Glenn

Racland whom she talked about constantly even though she didn't know him.

Clyde looked over the friend situation in the neighborhood and school, and decided to take his time. "I am my own best friend," he said one night at supper. "But there's a dog, Betty, who lives down the street and she shows promise."

"What kind of promise?" asked my mother, hoping to coax a clever remark out of Clyde.

"That's an expression," said Clyde. Clyde was not going to be a performer if he could help it.

My mother got the message. "Finish your meat, Clyde," she said, changing the subject. She was using psychology. Clyde hadn't even touched his meat yet.

"It's all fat," said Clyde. "Look at it."

"Someday Clyde's going to be a famous meat inspector," said Laurie.

"Ha, ha," said Clyde. "Just look at this meat. There's fat running straight through the middle of this piece. And this other piece is all fat. Fat, fat. Everywhere it's fat."

"Just eat it so the cow shouldn't have died in vain," said my mother. "And tomorrow I'll try a new butcher."

"What kind of cow was it?" asked Clyde. "I only know Guernsey and Jersey, and I think they're just for milk."

We never found out what kind of cow it was because

the telephone rang. Our telephone often gets busy in the middle of supper, which makes me think we are off schedule with the eating habits of the rest of the country.

"I'll get it," said Laurie.

"Good luck," said Clyde.

Laurie loved the telephone. In her life, it was the big link between what was and what could be. A date, a romance, a wrong number. But above all, it was HOPE.

The telephone kept on ringing. Laurie never rushed to pick up a receiver. "It looks anxious, you know."

At last, "Hello-o-o." Laurie's *o*'s took off in flight. "O-o-

o-o." They came down for a fast landing, and I knew the call wasn't for her.

"It's for you, Abby," she said, as if I had just committed a capital crime.

It was Hutch.

"What are you doing?" she asked.

"Eating supper."

"Well, come over right after. It's important."

"O.K."

I hung up.

Some words don't register with me. Like "important." It's a word that most people take advantage of, so it didn't mean much to me.

In this case it should have. I soon found out that Hutch had used exactly the right word.

Chapter
2

I finished supper. I never went over to Hutch's house hungry. ("Have some alfalfa sprouts, Abby.")

I also never went over there with dirty hands. ("Dirt under the fingernails. A rich breeding place for all kinds of germs.")

I never chewed gum in her house. ("Too much sugar in it, Abby. Bad for the teeth. Try sugarless.")

Not only Hutch, but her family as well were what I would call health conscious. It was their way of looking at things and maybe they were right. They certainly were unselfish about it, being concerned with other people's health as well as their own. I always felt guilty when I came back from Hutch's house and ate a piece of cake.

When I got to Hutch's house she took me immediately to her room. She closed the door. She didn't wait for me to sit down.

"Abby," she said, "I'm running away from home."

"What?"

"And I decided to tell someone about it. *You*. It's like making out a will. Someone should know if anything were to happen."

"Are you planning to die?"

"No, but I don't want to just disappear without *anyone* knowing where I am. Besides, I need your help because I'm planning to disappear without anyone noticing I've disappeared."

"How can you do that?"

"There is a way."

"Oh?"

"You'd have to run away, too."

"Who? Me?"

"Yes, *you*. Think about it. Have you *ever* left home on your own?"

"Twice. I made it the second time I tried. I went to visit an aunt fifteen miles away. I left a note for my folks."

"Weren't they mad?"

"What do you think? My aunt calmed them down, though. She told them I was asserting my independence. That's the way my aunt talks."

"What happened the first time you ran away?"

"Well, I thought I'd see how far I could get on my own."

"And?"

"I didn't get far at all. Half a dozen people reported to my mother that they had seen me alone two blocks from home."

"Why in the world did they do that?"

"Because I was four years old, that's why."

"Then you never *really* ran away from home," Hutch said.

"Yeah, those two times. I just told you."

"But when you're four years old it doesn't count. And going to your aunt's. That's nothing. Your running-away record is strictly blah, Abby."

"What's yours?"

"Blah, too. But not for long."

"You're serious about this?"

"Sure."

"Hutch, you haven't thought this through. We'd be playing hooky from school."

"School?" said Hutch. "Monday's Memorial Day.

There's no school. And anyway we'll be back Monday noon at the latest."

"You're going too fast for me, Hutch. How could we be back by Monday noon when it's almost Sunday now? How far could we get?"

"Not far," said Hutch. "That's the neat part of my plan. We don't have to waste time traveling."

"We don't?"

"No, there's a place that's very—er—convenient."

Hutch was speaking very slowly, spacing out her words to make them sound important.

"We'd—er—we'd do it together, Abby."

"Do what together?"

"Spend a night in the Lancelot model home."

"You're kidding!"

"Why do people always say you're kidding when they know the other person isn't? Of any kind of running away, this offers the biggest challenge. We'd be right near home all the time, but nobody would know it."

"How do you know they wouldn't?"

"I've worked on this idea a long time. You'll have to trust me. Look, it's much less dangerous than hitchhiking somewhere."

"I wasn't planning to hitchhike anywhere."

"Well, it's still less dangerous than hitchhiking."

Hutch was very good at influencing people by compar-

ing something she wanted them to do with something that was completely beside the point and dangerous. I caught on to her little trick soon after I met her, and she knew it. But that didn't stop her for a minute.

Still, I liked this idea of running away to a model home. It was different and it was convenient. I wondered if it was illegal. The public was invited to visit the model homes, and that's all we'd be doing. Visiting. Of course the public wasn't really invited to stay overnight. But then again they weren't told they couldn't.

I wondered why Hutch was so eager to run away. I wanted to ask, but I knew Hutch wouldn't tell me until she was good and ready.

Besides, I had my own decision to make. Should I go with Hutch? Shouldn't I go with Hutch? And why was I asking myself these questions anyway? I already knew what I would do. I already knew that I do not have one of the world's great positive personalities. I could tell Hutch that I wasn't going, but at the very moment I was telling her that, I'd be laying the groundwork for her to talk me into going.

I said, "I'll do it."

Hutch simply said, "Good." But I knew she meant "Great." She usually tried to keep her emotions under control. She once told me that you can get an ulcer if you don't. Or maybe she said if you do.

She leaned toward me and said, "We leave—" Then she stopped and I saw why. Her mother was standing in the doorway.

She said to Hutch, "Did you take the garbage out yet? There's no collection over the holiday, but at least we should get the stuff into the garage. The house is starting to reek."

Then she said, "Hello, Abby" to me.

That wasn't unusual. Mrs. Hutchins hardly ever said hello at once. First she'd mention some project or happening that had nothing to do with her visitor, and when she had finished, she'd get around to such minor things as saying hello. She never seemed quite to connect with other people, including Hutch.

But Mrs. Hutchins had an excuse for being unconnected. Mr. Hutchins went on a lot of business trips, and Mrs. Hutchins was left with all the responsibilities. Like Hutch. I think Hutch could have helped her mother more than she did, but I didn't tell that to Hutch. Hutch had her reason, and I knew what it was. Mrs. Hutchins is what I call a scorecard mother, always commenting on how Hutch does everything and comparing her with other kids. Mrs. Hutchins is not the only scorecard mother in the world. Probably most mothers have some scorecard in them, but they don't work at it full time the way Mrs. Hutchins does.

I said, "Hello, Mrs. Hutchins. I think your house smells good just the way it is."

That was undoubtedly one of the silliest things I've ever said. I had never smelled Hutch's house. I wasn't smelling Hutch's house now. But whenever she and her mother were together I seemed to have to say something to help Hutch.

Mrs. Hutchins said, "It would smell better if only Hutch were good at garbage." Then she left.

"I'm supposed to be the complete garbage collector," said Hutch. "Perfecto, you know."

"I'll help you take it out," I said. "And then we can get back to what we were talking about."

"The garbage can wait," said Hutch. "As I was saying, we leave tomorrow. Be careful how you dress. Dress medium. If you dress *up*, your family will be suspicious that you're going some place special. But if you dress *down*, the salesmen in the model home will get suspicious that you live in the neighborhood and came in to fool around."

"I thought you said that nobody would see us."

"They'll see us walk in, that's all. Then they'll forget about us. The salesmen who used to know us are gone. There've been two turnovers since Fast-talking Frank. Remember him? He sold your folks and my folks. He retired to Florida."

"What do we pack?"

"Nothing," said Hutch.

"Shouldn't we bring pajamas and a toothbrush?"

"You're going to walk in with a bag of pajamas? Forget it. I've got the toothbrushing problem taken care of. Also the food problem. But be sure to eat a good breakfast tomorrow. Breakfast should supply a major part of the day's nutritional requirements. Want to eat breakfast here? My mother will make us some cereal."

When Mrs. Hutchins makes cereal, it doesn't mean that she simply cooks it. She starts with the raw materials, all health foods, some of them grown in her organic garden in the back yard. She chooses and mixes and *then* she cooks. Right now I knew she was on a seaweed-extract kick.

"No, thanks just the same," I said, passing up the chance to eat what was probably the world's most uncontaminated breakfast.

"O.K. then, come over right after breakfast. You'll eat lunch here."

"I can eat at home easily. Your mother doesn't have to bother."

"I want you here right after breakfast tomorrow," said Hutch. "Otherwise you might let our plan slip. Now look, tell your folks that you're going to my house and will be home at noon on Monday. That's the truth, too. You just leave out that you're spending the night at the Lancelot."

"What are you telling your folks?"

"That I'm going to your house and will be back Monday noon."

"Couldn't you tell them that, even if I didn't go? Why do you need me?"

Hutch shrugged. "O.K. I don't have the nerve to run away alone. But it's a good plan, isn't it?"

Hutch's plan was neat and tidy. We often slept at each other's house, no questions asked. There was never any extra work for our parents because I slept in my sleeping bag and Hutch slept in the bed, no matter whose house it was. She wasn't allowed to sleep next to floors.

Hutch and I played a business-as-usual game of chess. Hutch and I were always playing chess. I remembered how she had first conned me into learning the game.

"It's a sharp game," she had said as she sat me down one day across a table and started putting knights and pawns and stuff on the chessboard. "Chess helps you to

think intelligently. Precisely. Vertically. Horizontally. And diagonally."

"I think O.K. now, Hutch."

"My mother taught me how to play, and her mother taught her. Once you learn you can start your own family tradition."

"My family already has traditions, Hutch. Cranberry pilgrims on Thanksgiving, gingerbread cookies on the first day of fall, and a red, white and blue flag-cake on the Fourth of July."

"Abby, your traditions will wreck your teeth. Chess will improve your mind."

"I give up."

Now I like chess, and once in a great while I beat Hutch. But not today. Today I wasn't concentrating. After our game I went home. I told my parents that I wanted to go to Hutch's house the next morning, and I wouldn't be back until Monday noon. They said it was fine with them. I went to bed. My bed is nice, but plain.

Tomorrow night I would be sleeping in style. Somewhere, in the spiffy rooms of the Lancelot model home, there was a spiffy bed waiting for me.

Chapter
3

The next morning I ate a breakfast that I was sure would not supply a major part of the day's nutritional requirements. I grabbed two doughnuts and a glass of milk. I was anxious to get started.

It was a problem to "dress medium." Most of my "medium" clothes were medium messy. So I picked out my next-to-newest jeans that had only two tiny holes just getting started. I hoped Hutch wouldn't notice them.

I made sure that my sleeping bag was stashed behind

some equipment in a basement closet. Then I went to Hutch's house.

She stared at me. "You mean you're going dressed that way? You look like a target."

"What do you mean, a target?"

"My father has this theory that some people dress so horribly that they give the impression of living permanently on a park bench, surviving on peanuts dropped for the pigeons. He says that these people get taken advantage of. They become targets for troublemakers."

"Look, Hutch, most kids look like targets. I'm sorry about my clothes, but I don't want to go back now."

"O.K. O.K. I wish you were thinner. You could wear something of mine."

We played chess until Hutch announced, "Lunchtime. At last I've got you for lunch."

Lunch was a Mother Hutchins Special: brown rice, sunflower lettuce, and steamed asparagus and mushrooms flavored with seaweed salt. Dessert was something made from vanilla beans, Irish moss and organic black mission figs.

"Eat as much as you want," said Hutch.

I couldn't do that and still be polite. As far as food is concerned, the world is against me anyway. Because of my allergies, I'm not supposed to eat peanut butter, nuts, strawberries, or anything chocolate. That takes care of most of the foods I like. What that doesn't take care of,

the orthodontist does. Because of my braces, I can't have popcorn, carbonated beverages, taffy apples or hard candy.

Mrs. Hutchins was standing at the head of the table. She smiled at us and said she had just come in from a bicycle ride and the weather was beautiful, and then she said hello to me and to Hutch.

Suddenly she asked, "Do you help your mother around the house?"

"Me?" I asked, stalling for time.

Mrs. Hutchins smiled again and looked around the room.

"I don't see anybody else here I would address that question to unless there's a gremlin hiding in the wood-work," she said.

I said, "I don't see any gremlins. Do you, Hutch?"

Hutch didn't answer.

I said, "Well, I help some, but not as much as Hutch."

"How about homework? Do you do much homework?"

"Well, I guess I do some, but probably not as much as Hutch."

"Hutch is marvelous in Social Studies," said Mrs. Hutchins. "You're in her class, aren't you? She's probably the best in her class."

Hutch squirmed because she knew she wasn't. How to help her?

I said, "Oh, well, Hutch isn't really *that* good."

"Who's better?" asked Mrs. Hutchins.

I said, "I don't know," even though I knew. About half the class. If only Mrs. Hutchins weren't so proud and unproud of Hutch in such definite ways.

Mrs. Hutchins sat down and talked to us about her garden, and it was interesting, and the rest of the meal was fine. If you didn't count the food.

Mrs. Hutchins started to load the dishwasher. I nudged Hutch and we helped her. She watched us very carefully, which made me sure I would drop a dish at any moment.

"A good job, girls," she said when we were finished.

Hutch and I went to her room. "When do we leave?" I asked.

"Not yet," said Hutch. "The Lancelot closes at five. We'll leave here about four. It might take us a while to get inside."

"I don't know what you mean, Hutch."

"I know you don't," said Hutch. "Let's play chess."

"Chess now?"

"What else?"

So we played chess.

At exactly four o'clock Hutch said, "I'll be back in two minutes and then we'll leave. We're going to walk over to the Lancelot in a natural way. Everything's natural until suddenly it's not natural."

Hutch left the room. She came back quickly and stood in the doorway.

"Let's go," she said.

As we walked along, I said, "You look fat today, Hutch. Bulgy."

"Just a few provisions I stuffed in my pockets," said Hutch. "I told you I'd take care of the food."

"Hutch, are these provisions *health food* provisions?"

"Trust me," said Hutch.

"Hutch, nobody in their right mind runs away from home with health food."

"Trust me," said Hutch again. "Abby, you know we're advertised in the *New York Times* today. Open house at Camelot. Maybe there'll be hundreds of people. It's a holiday weekend. Maybe there'll be thousands."

"Hutch, what kind of book are you carrying?"

"Say, you're really looking me over. A target has no right to make remarks about how other people look or what they're carrying."

"All right. But can I ask why we're walking along in plain sight of whoever might pass by or look out of a window? If our families find out we're gone, they'll ask the neighbors if they've seen us."

"People might see us, Abby, but they won't really see us because we're doing what we should be doing where we should be doing it. Walking down our own street. I told you before that we're being natural. Natural doesn't register. Natural is almost invisible."

"Hutch, could almost invisible me ask almost invisble you one more question? Why did you pick the Lancelot?"

"Because I live in a Lancelot and the model home is identical to my house. I know all the rooms and closets and where every door leads to."

Hutch and I turned one corner and then another. The three model homes are located on Forest Road which is parallel to Oakdale Road. As we walked toward the model homes, I could see the back of my house and Hutch's house on Oakdale Road. I hardly ever saw my house from this view. It seemed very far away.

Chapter 4

Forest Road was full of cars. And people talking, gazing at the houses and making their way up the walks. Each of the three houses had a "Model" sign on the outside. The builders also should have supplied "Not a Model" signs for the people who were already living in Camelot houses. At odd hours people have rung our doorbell, wanting to look inside. Sometimes they knew it wasn't a model home, but after driving to Camelot and finding the model homes were closed, they weren't quite ready to give up. "May I use your telephone, please?" they'd ask. Or "Would you mind if we just took a quick peek inside your house? We drove here from Carmel, California." The same thing happens at Hutch's house. Maybe the builders owed Hutch and me some hospitality.

We stopped in front of the Lancelot. "We now attach ourselves," said Hutch.

"Attach ourselves? To what?"

"To people," said Hutch. "Stray kids like us would get kicked out immediately. We'll find a couple of people or a small group we can fit in with, and we'll walk in with them or very close to them. As you walk in, think *I am part of this family. They are my people. I am their people.*"

Hutch and I waited. But it was like waiting for space in a busy revolving door. Every time we saw a good chance, it was over before we could act.

"Let's take these people," said Hutch finally.

A man and woman were coming up the walk. As they got closer, I saw that they were quite old. "We're grand-daughters," Hutch whispered. We ran to the side of the couple as they were opening the front door. We were in such a rush that we pushed them. They stopped.

The man spoke. "Look here, girls, do you know how many years you've got to make it through this door? My wife and I don't have nearly as much time. Now stand back and let us through."

The man and woman walked into the house. Hutch and I followed. It would have been more conspicuous to turn back than to keep going, and anyway we were conversationally attached to them.

"We just had a family fight," Hutch whispered to me.

We walked sort of in back of, sort of beside the couple into the big entrance hall. They either didn't see us or pretended not to. They stopped, so we stopped. They were admiring the view. Hutch and I had been in the house a few times before when our parents were deciding on their houses. But every time I was astonished all over again. The house, the brochure said, was decorated in the style of the Camelot of the Middle Ages with tapestries and some heavy beams and stone floors. But most of the stuff looked phony—shiny and plastic.

Hutch and I stuck with "grandfather" and "grandmother." They went into the kitchen. A salesman was sitting at the kitchen table with some papers. I knew he was a salesman because he was dressed up. It seemed to me that about seventy-five percent of the people walking around were dressed like targets. I didn't mention that to Hutch. When I grow up, I would like a job where I could always dress like a target and get away with it. Maybe I'll be a writer like my father.

"This is where we'll be eating," Hutch whispered. "Come on. Let's move. Follow me."

"What about Grandpa and Grandma?"

"They've served their purpose," said Hutch. "And grandchildren like us they don't need."

We walked down a hall. The Lancelot is a ranch-type house, and on the main floor there's a kitchen, dining room, living room, den, three bedrooms and two bathrooms. Downstairs is a basement. We passed a couple of bedrooms and a bathroom and a den. Another salesman was sitting at a desk in the den.

"Let's go to the master bedroom," said Hutch. "We'll hide there until the Lancelot closes for the night."

We stopped in front of a huge bedroom. It had very dark walls, and the bed and chairs and chests looked old.

But we knew they were new. There was something odd
about that. The room seemed to be saying, "I am old on
purpose."

There was a Plexiglas chain strung across the doorway.

"That's to protect the furniture from undesirables like
us," Hutch whispered.

Some people were standing in front of the chain. Hutch and I stood back by ourselves. "Well, here's where we hang out," she said.

"Where here?"

"Under the bed."

"What? I am not going to hide under a bed. It's not even healthy under there. I'm surprised at you, Hutch."

"I adapt to conditions," said Hutch. "Under a bed is the only place nobody ever looks because there's nothing to see. People going through model homes are peekers. Most of them aren't even interested in building a house. They just come and poke around. It's an established pastime in the United States. *Veni, vidi, vici.* I came, I saw, I conquered my curiosity."

"I thought you chose the Lancelot because you knew the rooms so well. Now the only hiding place you can come up with is under a bed. Hey, how about the basement? It's gigantic."

"And exposed," said Hutch.

"How about the furnace room?" I asked.

"The furnace room is a very popular place for people who are seriously thinking of buying a house," said Hutch. "You don't get as many lookers as in the other rooms, but you get *scrutinizers*. That's worse."

"You win," I said.

"That means under the bed," said Hutch.

"Under the bed," I said.

We waited until several groups had come and gone and we were finally alone. We scooted under the chain and crawled under the bed.

It was hot under the bed. And dark. And dusty. Poor Hutch, surrounded by pollution.

We whispered to each other. We weren't afraid to do that because some of the time we were alone and the rest of the time there were voices of other people to cover ours. Nobody unhooked the chain or crawled under it. Nobody, that is, except Phillips N. Jameson.

Phillips N. Jameson, five years old, and his parents stopped at the bedroom. After a few minutes his parents left. Phillips N. Jameson ducked under the chain, came over to the bed, lifted up the bedspread and peered at Hutch and me.

"Me Phillips N. Jameson," he shouted, and he laughed. Fiendishly. "You girls. You girls." He ran out of the room shouting, "Girls under the bed, girls under the bed!"

"Nobody will believe him," said Hutch. "He's too young. You've seen those movies. Little kids warn their parents about something that's horrible and fantastic and true. It takes over an hour before anybody believes the little kid."

"In the movies," I said.

Hutch and I lay still. Now we were afraid to talk. I guess about fifteen minutes passed. Someone came and turned off the lights in the room. The Lancelot was closing for the night.

And as it happened, nobody did believe Phillips N. Jameson.

Chapter
5

We stayed under the bed. The house got quieter and quieter, and finally we could hear only the two salesmen. Then we heard the front door close and two cars drive off. We waited a few more minutes. The house seemed completely still. We crept out from under the bed.

"Vertical again," said Hutch. And she stretched.

"Now what?" I asked.

"How about some supper?"

"What do you have in mind, and where?"

"The kitchen is where and you'll soon see what," said Hutch.

The kitchen looked lonely. It was a long room with gleaming equipment and a tremendous sliding glass door, and there was a view of endless trees. Hutch immediately pulled the draperies over the door.

"Privacy," she said.

"Concealment, you mean."

"Oh, I'm pretty sure that no one can see us," she said. "But why take a chance."

"Can we turn on a light?"

"There's a small light on the stove. That's all we need for now, and I don't think it can be seen from the outside. I brought a flashlight for later so we won't have to turn on lights." Hutch spoke with a kind of I-crossed-this-bridge-before-we-came-to-it authority. "And now," she said, "it's time for supper."

We went to the kitchen table. It was empty except for an ashtray overflowing with cigarette butts. Hutch dumped them into the sink and ran the disposal. She even did that with authority. "Did you know," she said, "that cigarette smoking adversely affects the body's ability to utilize Vitamin C? Vitamin C, along with Vitamin D, helps the body excrete poisons. But don't take excessive amounts of Vitamin C or D or you're in trouble."

"Hutch, will we be having Vitamin C, D, or any other vitamins for supper? Come on, did you pack that seaweed stuff?"

"Let's sit down and make ourselves comfortable," said Hutch.

We sat down at the table. The chairs felt crackly and hard.

"They're made to look at, not to sit on," said Hutch.

She put the book which she had been carrying on the kitchen table and opened it. The book was a box and it was full of candy bars.

"I got this box in a novelty store," she said. "The crim-

inal element knows about this kind of box and uses it for shoplifting. It should be banned like cigarettes."

For a minute I couldn't believe the book-box. But for five minutes I couldn't believe the candy bars. Hutch with candy bars! An even dozen of them.

"Hutch, all these sweets. Your teeth! This looks like a cavity convention."

"I adapt to conditions," she said, biting into a chewy chocolate bar. "What's the matter?"

"I'm not allowed to eat candy bars," I said.

"Abby, all rules are suspended for the night."

"I can't get over you, Hutch. Anyway, I've got problems you don't have. Like braces and allergies."

Hutch stood up and emptied her pockets. They were full of little cellophane-wrapped packages of cake. "Have some pound cake. And some coffee cake," she said, tossing the cakes onto the table. With all the candy bars and cakes spread around, the table looked as if a full night's worth of Halloween collections had been dumped on it.

I ate a piece of pound cake which tasted stale. Hutch was eating one candy bar after another. I had never seen such enjoyment in my life. We both knew that her chances of getting sick were increasing with every bite she took, but she seemed intent upon chewing her way to some sort of twelve-bar victory.

I tried to slow her down. "Hutch," I said, "what are we having for breakfast tomorrow?"

Hutch stopped in the middle of a chew. "Candy and cake," she said.

"What candy? I'm having *some* cake for supper. You're eating *all* the candy. Hutch, you're on a collision course with cavities. And remember, too much chocolate isn't good for the heart."

"You learned that from me," said Hutch. "I'll stop after the next bar."

"I'm thirsty," I said. "Do you suppose there's anything to drink in the refrigerator?"

"Nope. The refrigerator isn't plugged in."

I opened the refrigerator. It was empty. And warm.

"You can get water from the faucet. That works," said Hutch. "Cup your hands."

"Why don't you write a survival manual for a model home?" I said.

"There's no market for that kind of literature," said Hutch. "Your father's a writer. You should know."

Hutch stopped eating. She drooped over the table like someone who had lost all interest in everything in the world, everything except a terrible stomach full of crunchy, wunchy, chewy, chocolaty yecch.

It's not fair to take advantage of people when they're down, but just the same I said, "Hutch, why did you really want to spend a night at the Lancelot?"

"Because it was there," said Hutch, holding her stomach.

"Seriously, Hutch."

"Seriously? All right, Abby. The truth is that I wanted to do something just because *I* wanted to do it."

"Well sure, Hutch. What other reason is there to want to do something?"

Hutch laughed. "Are you kidding? How about to get

recognition, rewards and all that kind of stuff?"

"Oh."

"See, Abby, this isn't the usual thing like math or history or chess. This is different. I made this plan up, I worked it out and now *I've* done it. And that's what counts. That's all that counts. Hutch knowing what Hutch wants to do and doing it."

Hutch stood up and I knew she didn't want to talk about it any more.

"Well, let's walk off our supper," she said.

"What about the food on the table? And the wrappers on the floor?" I asked.

"Tomorrow morning we'll clean up," said Hutch. "We'll even make the bed. We'll leave the place spick-and-span."

"What time are we leaving tomorrow?"

"We'll clear out of here by nine. The Lancelot doesn't open until ten."

"Then we're not leaving the way we came—natural?"

"No, what if one of the salesmen remembers seeing us come in the day before?"

I nodded. Hutch turned off the stove light and started to leave the kitchen.

"Let's watch TV," I said.

"What's the matter with you?" said Hutch. "You can watch TV at home. And besides, this TV set doesn't work. In model homes some things work, and some don't. I came in here weeks ago and tried everything out. I pressed buttons and turned knobs and flicked switches whenever there was no one around."

We walked through all the rooms. We had to go under some chains to do it. Finally we sat down in the den. The den had the TV set that didn't work, as well as more chairs that weren't meant to be sat on. Hutch sat down at the desk which the salesman had used in the afternoon. On the desk were magazines with names like *Realty Today* and *Better Building*. There was also a nameplate on the desk with the name Lucar Properties, Inc. in gold.

Hutch leaned on the desk. "I am president, vice president, secretary, treasurer and chairman of the board of Lucar Properties, Inc.," she said. "We build houses. Would you like a house, madam? We have three handsome models to choose from in glorious Camelot."

I stood in front of the desk. "I would be most pleased to have a house," I said. "But my name is Merlin and I am far too wise to buy any of yours. However, I will be glad to borrow a bedroom. Madam president, vice president, secretary, treasurer and chairman of the board, let's go to bed."

Chapter 6

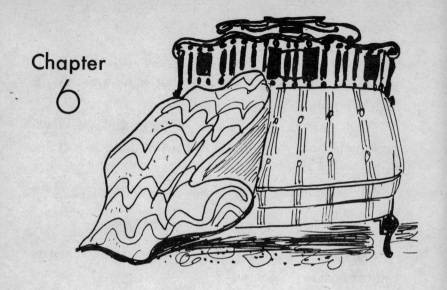

We went to the bedroom and stood in front of the chain like two spectators waiting for something to happen on the other side.

"It's really not dark enough to go to bed yet," said Hutch.

"I know, but there's not much to do when you can't use the electricity. Anyway, I'm anxious to try out this big bed."

We ducked under the chain and pulled back the heavy

bedspread. Under the bedspread was a mattress.

"No sheets," I said. "Nothing but a mattress. We'll both be button-faced by morning."

"We'll survive," said Hutch. "I guess they didn't expect anybody to sleep in the bed. Everything is only for looks around here."

"My sleeping bag at home suddenly seems very inviting," I said.

"Are you quitting?"

"No, I always wanted to sleep in a medieval twentieth-century bed. Let's get ready."

"There are toothbrushes and toothpaste in the bathroom," said Hutch. "Courtesy of the management."

"But we can't use those," I said. "They're just for decoration."

Hutch was already in the bathroom squeezing out toothpaste. "It's real toothpaste," she said. "And the toothbrushes are real, too. And the soap. And the towels are soft. And the plumbing works. I'd give these accommodations a four-star rating. If there were sheets." Hutch started to clean her teeth. She stopped. "And some good chairs," she said. "And a few other things. Make it two stars."

I cleaned my teeth. Even though I squeezed the toothpaste tube very gently, it now had a bent, used look. There were two towels in the room. Hutch had already used one. I couldn't use the same towel as Hutch. I'd

heard her say often enough it was like wiping your hands on somebody else's germs. But I had just used her tooth-paste tube and she hadn't seemed to mind. The very same toothpaste tube she'd be putting her brush on tomorrow morning.

What was going on anyway? First, I couldn't believe that Hutch had actually lain on that dusty floor under the bed, and had chucked those candy bars into her mouth one after the other. Dust and candy bars. And now a shared toothpaste tube. I wanted to congratulate her, but I kept my mouth shut.

Not only had something unusual happened to Hutch, but we were turning the Lancelot into a mess. The bedroom with the bedspread sloppily pulled back, the bathroom with towels drooping from the towel rack, dirt-covered soap on the sink, a toothpaste tube and cap and toothbrushes lying every which way on the counter—the house looked used. And now I knew what people admired most about model homes. They admired what wasn't used. Beds that weren't slept in, sinks that weren't washed in, tables that weren't eaten on.

Hutch climbed into bed. "The mattress itches," she said. "Let's sleep on top of the bedspread."

The bedspread itched, too. But it was softer than the mattress. "This is the biggest bed I've ever been in," I said. "It's also the worst. I give this establishment a one-star rating, subject to withdrawal at any time. Well, when you scratch, scratch quietly. Good night."

"Say, Abby, what do you suppose Lucar stands for? You know, businessmen stick parts of their family names together and make company names out of them. Maybe the builder's daughter is named Lulu and his son is named Cary. Or his father is Ludwig and his mother is Carmen. Or maybe his dog is Lucretia and his cat is Archibald."

"Hutch, the builder's name is *Luther Carstairs*."

"I know," Hutch said. "I just wanted to stay up."

"Good night, Hutch."

"No, not good night," said Hutch. She sat up in bed. "Abby, do you know something? I did it. I did it. I'm here. It was my idea. Nobody else's. I carried out my plan. I'm a success."

"I know it, Hutch. I'm here with you. And now you can go to sleep knowing you've done it. And I can go to sleep knowing you've done it. And I'd like to go to sleep now."

"I have to stay up," said Hutch. "Because the whole thing is starting to slip away from me. Because it will be morning and we'll be gone and even while I'm talking it's starting to go away and I have to keep it."

"But you've already done what you wanted to do," I said. "Nobody can take that away from you."

"It's slipping away in the dark," said Hutch. And she got out of bed and turned on the bedroom light. Then she ran out and turned on the hall lights and the kitchen light.

I got up and ran after her. "What are you doing? You can't keep these lights on. What if somebody sees them?"

"It's a celebration," Hutch said. "What's a celebration without lights."

"We'll be caught," I said. "We'll be caught for sure."

I went back to bed and wrapped myself in the bedspread. Including my head. Then I heard a car drive up. I got out of the bedspread and went to the window. I peeked out. I saw a police car.

One of the things that my parents like most about Shady Landing is the sight of police cars going by now and then. It makes them feel as if their street, their house, they themselves really matter. I liked it, too, although I didn't care as much as my parents. But now I had very strong feelings about the police car. All I wanted it to do was drive away.

Hutch came running into the bedroom. "It's the police," she said.

"I know. Quick, let's turn off the lights." I ran for the bedroom switch.

"No!" shouted Hutch. "Don't touch that. If they see lights go off, they'll know someone is inside. Like this,

maybe they'll think the lights were left on for the night on purpose."

"O.K.," I said. "You're the boss."

"Shh," said Hutch.

We heard footsteps on the front stairs. Then we heard the doorknob being tried. And we saw moving lights from a flashlight. Then we heard footsteps going away. Soon we heard the back door being tried. Then, in a few minutes, we heard the car drive away.

"I can't stand this any more," I said to Hutch. "I'm going to sleep and try to forget where I am."

"I saved us," said Hutch. "And it was completely spur of the moment. Ad lib, you might say."

I crawled into bed. "I'm asleep. Don't talk to me. Turn off the light."

"I can't," said Hutch. "What if the police car drives by?"

"You're right," I said. "Unfortunately."

I fell asleep with the lights on.

I woke up to the sound of crunch crunch. Hutch must have turned the lights off because it was dark. She was sitting up in bed eating candy bars.

"Hutch!"

"Yes?"

"Hutch!"

"You already said that. I was so hungry I woke up.

Aren't you hungry? I brought you some cake in case you woke up. I dropped some of it on the kitchen floor and I knocked the ashtray off the table and broke it. Well, the only good ashtray is a broken ashtray."

"I'm trying to sleep. Can't you eat in the kitchen?"

"Sure, but I can do that at home. I'm not allowed to eat in bed at home."

"Hutch, you just said the magic word. Home. That's where I'm going. Now."

"You'd leave me in the middle of the night?"

"You come, too. You said you've already succeeded. We're here, we didn't get caught. Now we can go home."

"No, I can't. It's not finished until I stay the night," said Hutch. "But you can go if that's the way you feel."

Hutch's voice sounded different. As if it were taking orders from a new person, a person who didn't like me. "Do what you want," it said. She lay down and turned her back to me.

Now she was sore at me. But if I stayed the night, we would be friends again in the morning. I decided to stay. I wrapped part of the bedspread around me. I felt hot-cold-prickly all at the same time. I kept turning one way and then the other. Maybe Hutch wouldn't be mad if I left? After all, the hardest part of the plan was over with.

I couldn't find my socks in the dark. I got my shoes and groped my way to the front door. I unlocked it and left. When I was outside I stopped. I tried the door but it had locked behind me. Maybe I would have gone back if it hadn't.

Walking home was spooky. My feet felt clammy without my socks, and my hands felt clammy, too.

It was easy to get into my house. We kept our back yard lighted at night. And we kept a key to the basement door buried in a bed of pebbles. After just a little clawing, I found it.

I let myself in quietly. Fortunately I could see by the outside light. I took my sleeping bag out of the closet, unrolled it, and got inside. Ah, a thousand, a million times better than the itchy bed at the Lancelot. But now I didn't feel sleepy. I had deserted my friend. Hutch had needed me to run away with, and she needed me to stay.

I needed her, too. Hutch had really done a lot for me. I'm not what you call daring. I think I'm a bit of a coward. I don't care to go to school without every last inch of my homework done. And I would rather follow than lead. Not only would I rather be second than first, I would rather be third than second. Hutch had been working on me to make me bolder. I started to think of bold things I could do and it put me to sleep.

I woke up after eight. I had the same breakfast as the day before, only faster. I had to get in and out of the kitchen and out of the house that I wasn't supposed to be in. Fortunately everyone was sleeping late because it was a holiday.

I put my sleeping bag back in the closet and left the house.

I got my bike and rode down Oakdale Road over to

Forest Road. I was on the lookout for Hutch. I hoped she had cleared out of the house by now, but I was afraid to call for her at her own house to find out. I rode around to the side of the Lancelot, got off my bike and ran up to the window of the master bedroom. But I couldn't see inside.

"Hutch," I called.

No answer. I called again. Louder. No answer. I got on my bike, rode down the street and stopped. I turned around and watched the house and waited. Any minute now Hutch might come out of the Lancelot.

A salesman arrived. Well, if you're not out now, Hutch, you're in trouble. Another salesman came, and soon after that, a police car arrived.

Chapter 7

Two policemen got out of the car and went into the Lancelot. They were there for a long time. Then they came out with the two salesmen. I felt like cheering when I saw that Hutch wasn't with them. The policemen checked the windows, studied the ground, poked bushes and made notes. They walked around the house, examining it like two doctors. Then they left.

Hutch *must* be home safe. Or was she in the Lancelot lying under the bed with the dust and candy wrappers?

There was only one way left to find out.

I rode over to Hutch's house. I went to the back door. Hutch usually answered the back door, and Mrs. Hutchins usually answered the front door. I hadn't thought about it until just then, but maybe some people are naturally front-door people and some are back-door people.

Nobody answered the back door. I went around to the front door. No answer there either. Wasn't anybody home? Had the police been there first? Or was Hutch inside—furious at me? I would have given anything for just a little glimpse of her.

I saw Clyde walking toward me with Betty. They ran up to me. Betty was happy to see me. That's the great thing about dogs. They can be glad to see you when you haven't done anything to deserve it. I hoped Hutch would feel the same way when I found her.

Clyde said, "I borrowed Betty for the whole day, and I'm taking her to the parade. Want to come with us?"

The Memorial Day Parade. Maybe Hutch would be *there*.

"Sure," I said.

I left my bike at my house and walked with Clyde and Betty. As we walked Clyde said, "My feet sweat when I don't wear socks. Don't yours?"

"Sometimes," I said. Clyde was always noticing dumb things like no socks, unfranked stamps on mailed letters and the resemblance of a certain rock formation to his teacher's face.

The Memorial Day Parade is an annual event in Shady Landing. It had already started when we got to town. I watched the parade, and I watched the crowds watching it. I saw at least three girls who looked just like Hutch from the back but not the front.

I also saw Laurie and her friend Jill across the street talking to some boys. One of them was Glenn. Laurie meets Glenn! Glenn talks to Laurie! The miracle had happened. I hoped our family was allotted more than one miracle for the day, because I sure needed one.

Time and people went by. The veterans, the mayor, the Board of Trustees, Boy Scouts, Girl Scouts, school bands, volunteer firemen and policemen marched past me. But no Hutch.

Suddenly in the crowd at the curb I saw another girl who looked like Hutch from the back. And the front. It was Hutch.

I pushed my way to her. "Hutch! Hey, Hutch!"

She turned toward me and then turned away. She had chocolate smudges on her face.

"Hutch, am I glad to see you!" I said to the back of her head.

She didn't answer.

"Hutch, I'm so glad you're out of there. And I'm sorry I left. Really I'm sorry. I did a rotten thing, O.K.?"

The back of her head made a strange movement, as if nodding in agreement.

"Are we friends again, Hutch?"

Hutch turned around and looked me square in the face. "Get lost," she said.

"But. . . ."

She turned away again.

"Hutch, what's the big deal? I said I was sorry. Why are you so mad?"

Hutch turned back and glared at me. "I'm mad because what was important to me—what was maybe the most important thing that I ever did—didn't mean anything to you. You walked out on me because of a noisy candy bar and an itchy bedspread or some other stupid reason. A real friend wouldn't do that. A real friend wouldn't leave if her life depended on it. A real friend is something you're *not*."

"Look, Hutch," I said. "You're judging by what a friend like *you* would do, not a friend like *me*. I *am* your

66 ■

real friend, but I'm *my* kind of real friend because that's the only kind of friend I know how to be. I'm a scared real friend. You're a brave real friend. What makes you brave makes me poop out. Understand?"

Then I walked away because I wanted to think. When I was explaining to Hutch, I was explaining myself to myself, too.

I went back to Clyde and Betty, and watched the rest of the parade with them. But my mind was on Hutch. Maybe our friendship was over? Yet this wasn't the way friendships should end. Well, I supposed I could find a friend to replace Hutch. Still, why bother? Maybe I would just be independent and do things by myself. Maybe I would be better off on my own.

I was kidding myself, and I knew it.

The parade was over and we went home. My mother and father were in the garage painting furniture. They

said "Welcome home" to me, as they wiped some paint from themselves. Clyde told them about the parade. Then he went into the house to get some lunch for himself and Betty.

I was almost out of the garage, too, when my father said, "Did you hear about the mystery in Camelot?"

"Mystery? What mystery?"

"The Lancelot was vandalized last night under strange circumstances. Doris Appleby told us."

"Mrs. Appleby? How did she know about it?"

My mother said, "From the Oakdale Road grapevine. It surpasses any news service Reuters could ever have dreamed up."

Doris Appleby lives in an Excalibur a few houses away. She has a habit of calling up neighbors to report on what other neighbors are doing. There is also a Camelot Homeowners Association, called CHA, which is her strongest competition for dispatching information, but she belongs to it anyway.

I spoke up. "What do you mean, vandalized? And whatever you mean, do they know who did it?"

"All we got was a one-sentence bulletin," said my father. "I'm going down to the police station later to check on it."

My appetite for lunch immediately disappeared.

My father is interested in mysterious activities of any

type. He is a frequent visitor to police stations, hospitals and morgues. Whatever ideas he can pick up from real life, he uses in his books. I think there's some sort of machine in his brain that goes around and around and it mixes and blends everyone and everything, and pretty soon out comes a story.

All afternoon I waited for the local newspaper to come. When it did, I was the first in the family to pick it up. Would there be any mention of what had happened at the Lancelot? Maybe it was too insignificant to put in the paper.

On page 6, I found out it wasn't.

Chapter
8

MODEL HOME VANDALIZED

Lucar Properties, Inc., builder of the Camelot housing development in Shady Landing, reported to the police that the Lancelot model home on Forest Road had been vandalized sometime between the closing hour of 5 P.M. Sunday and the opening time of 10 A.M. today.

When salesmen Lynden S. Craig and Richard S. Andrew entered the Lancelot this morning, they found litter and broken glass, and the kitchen, master bedroom and bathroom were in disarray.

Police in a cruising patrol car last evening noticed that the lights in the model home were on. They checked doors and investigated the grounds but found nothing unusual.

This morning there were no signs of forcible entry, and since all windows and doors were locked, the police are unable to theorize as to the method of entry or the motive. An early check of the premises indicated that nothing had been taken.

Luther B. Carstairs, president of Lucar Properties, in a statement released to this newspaper, said, "Hoboes —homeless, sad, wandering tramps—found themselves a shelter for one night. No permanent damage was done, and we can replace the vandalized items at a cost of $10.63. But this country needs more well-built, economical, attractive houses such as the Camelot homes. If decent housing were available to everyone, people would not be tempted to occupy other people's property."

I read the article twice. I couldn't believe it the first time and I couldn't believe it the second time. The newspaper, which prints both local and world news, gave the Lancelot story twice as much space as the promotion of a bank vice president and about the same amount of space as the arrival of a chimpanzee at the Central Park Zoo.

And now what? Hutch would be calling me soon. People who are in trouble together can't afford to be enemies.

Hutch did not call me soon or even later, though I

knew she must have read the paper, just as I had. And she too would have heard the grapevine report.

But there was someone eager to talk about it. My father. He asked me if I was through with the newspaper. I gave it to him. He started to read it, commenting on items as he went along. Item Number Three: Vandalism at the Lancelot.

"I took a little stroll down to the police station this afternoon," he said. "This Lancelot business seems to have them stymied. They're thinking now that perhaps the intruders had started to rob the house and for some reason changed their mind. But certain factors have them puzzled."

"Certain factors?"

"Yes. They can understand the use of towels to perhaps get rid of fingerprints, but the used toothbrushes and toothpaste—well, what kind of burglar worries about cleaning his teeth on the job? Or I should say *their* teeth. Two toothbrushes were used."

"Two, really?"

"I told them I once had a similar situation in one of my books. Remember Queenie in *Wake Up Dead*? Queenie was a murderer, but she powdered her nose at the scene of the crime just as she did when she was at home. She couldn't break the habit just because she was committing murder."

"Habits are habits, I guess. What else did the police say?"

"They told me that numerous candy and cake wrappers were found in the kitchen and in the bed. And the bedspread looked like a restless elephant had slept on it. Which of course brings up the Goldilocks question."

"What's that?"

"That's the who-has-been-sleeping-in-my-bed angle." My father folded the newspaper. "Then again, none of this may be relevant," he said. "It's possible that the intruders deliberately made a mess in order to hide their real intentions."

"Well, yes, I suppose so. But what are the police going to do about it, Dad?"

"They didn't tell me and I didn't ask. But I know what I'd do. For openers I'd try to trace the candy and cake wrappers. I'd see if there were any mass purchases of cake and candy in the area recently."

Oh, Hutch, I hope you bought those sweets one at a time over a period of months. *Years!*

"Dad, what else would you do?"

"Want a list? Read the next chapter and find out."

"You mean you're putting this in a book?"

"I might. I'll see. Maybe I'll make Carstairs the villian if I can work it out. I'll change his name a bit so he won't sue. How do you like that Carstairs! He's turning the incident into a soapbox for himself and his housing development. For $10.63 he gets all that publicity."

"But isn't it bad publicity? Won't it scare people away?"

"No, it wasn't a murder. It wasn't even a robbery as far as anyone knows. And Carstairs gets himself a reputation as a defender of . . . of . . . ."

"Targets," I said.

"Targets? What do you mean?"

"Oh, nothing. Just an expression I once heard."

"Well, Carstairs can use a good image. Camelot is getting tired of waiting for him to come through on his promises. The water is still rusty, all the Guinevere roof gutters are inadequate, most of us have flooded basements every time it rains, and we still have no streetlights. CHA is meeting here tonight. I hope that something worthwhile comes out of it."

CHA has ten members, or if you count husbands and wives separately, it has twenty. Once a month, or oftener if necessary, they meet to discuss problems in the development. My father is secretary of the association.

When the meeting is at our house I usually hang around for some of it because it's kind of dramatic. People raise their voices or swear or say something colorful which I would never get to hear any other way. Also kids are welcome, anybody is welcome, anybody who can help fill up a room and is loyal to and willing to work for Camelot.

Even though there are kids around, these meetings are actually the big adult social thing in the development where everybody gets to know everybody else. Sort of. Their friendships are based on having a common enemy, flooded basements, missing streetlights, and the chance to get up and talk, talk, talk. Maybe when things settle down and people really begin to know each other, they'll have something better going for them. I hope so, because it's pretty sad this way.

After supper, my mother and father cleaned the house as if they were up for a Good Housekeeping award. Laurie and I helped them set up borrowed folding chairs in the basement. In Camelot, meetings always take place in basements.

Laurie, by the way, did not mention that she had met Glenn, and I didn't mention it. I was definitely in the mood to be a respecter of secrets.

The meeting was supposed to start at 8:30. At 9:00

five people had arrived. Mr. and Mrs. Alfred Tinker and their three children, Lonny, Lenny and Laura. Laura was an infant and fast asleep. Mr. and Mrs. Tinker didn't believe in baby-sitters. If you invited the Tinkers, you invited their children. The Tinkers sat down and looked lonesome. Next a bonanza. Seven people came, all grown up. Then two more. By 9:15, there were representatives of seven Camelot houses, and the meeting began.

I sat back in my chair which felt as uncomfortable as the Lancelot chairs. The president and vice president were absent. Mrs. Hutchins was the vice president. Her husband didn't come either. Very good. I didn't want them chatting with my parents about Hutch's night at my house and my parents chatting about my night at Hutch's house.

My father called the meeting to order. Mr. Tinker got up. Lonny and Lenny got up, too. I think they thought they were leaving. Mr. Tinker started to speak. Lonny and Lenny yawned and sat down.

"First of all, as chairman of the Floods Committee," Mr. Tinker began, "I want to say that it's a pleasure to see a basement full of people, not water."

Some of the people smiled and some frowned.

"*However*," said Mr. Tinker, "we have a sunny day, not Mr. Carstairs, to thank for this."

Everybody groaned.

"*However*, I *am* pleased to report that the average basement in Camelot now only floods a couple of inches as compared to a previous level of approximately three feet. Carstairs has succeeded in rerouting some of the water directly to the sewer instead of to our houses. *However*, the problem is still with us. I had another appointment with Carstairs two weeks ago, and told him that our basements are still flooding whenever it rains. He told me that he had made an appointment for the next week to meet with the Water and Sewer Department to discuss our drainage problems. So a week later I called the Water and Sewer Department. They told me they're meeting with the Village Engineer to discuss our problem."

"Why don't you skip all that and just call the mayor?" someone interrupted.

"I'm coming to that," said Mr. Tinker. "That's precisely what I did do. The mayor is going to discuss the matter with the Board of Trustees who will probably vote to take up the matter with Carstairs."

"Who will then say he will take up the matter with the Water and Sewer Department," I said to myself.

Mr. Tinker sat down. There was very loud mumbling and grumbling considering the small number of people in the room.

Other committee chairmen got up. It was the same story all over again with Mr. Carstairs and the village.

Then Doris Appleby got up. She was the Streetlights Liaison Person. I sort of admired Doris Appleby because she knew how to make a lot out of a little. I was almost in awe of her, in the same way that I was in awe of other special-ability people like counterfeiters and swindlers. Tonight she got up from her chair slowly, conspicuously, like an unfolding measuring stick. After she had completely unfolded, she spoke.

"What we've been hearing tonight, my fellow Camelot residents, is one unfortunate report after another.

Now, I've been an executive secretary for years, first in Poughkeepsie, then in Schenectady, and I've sat in on top management meetings and I've found that it is not necessarily the person who yells the loudest or the most often who gets heard. In Poughkeepsie, for example. . . ."

Doris always told parts of the story of her life before she made her point. Tonight's Poughkeepsie installment took only about five minutes. Then she said, "And so, I maintain that the person who gets heard is the person who yells the *cleverest*."

Unfortunately Doris was now yelling and so was the Tinker baby. But Doris went on. "You have placed your trust in me to obtain streetlights for the development. I have obtained a promise from Mr. Carstairs that we will have them as soon as possible. But no applause, please. 'As soon as possible' is an expression that brings out the snail in Mr. Carstairs. In addition, my task is extremely difficult because Mr. Carstairs doesn't have to give us streetlights until the streets are dedicated by the village, and the village doesn't have to dedicate the streets until all the houses are built."

There was more grumbling.

"We all know," she continued, "that it is dangerous to be without streetlights. Mr. Carstairs knows that, and the village knows that, but until today it was merely an abstract piece of information. But now *crime* has come to the development, and I feel that the absence of streetlights contributed to it. I'm referring, of course, to the vandalism at the Lancelot. I intend to use that incident for all it's worth to get us our streetlights *now*."

Suddenly I had the most tremendous respect for Hutch. For the project she had thought up. It had really caught on. There seemed to be something in it for almost

everybody. For Mr. Carstairs, for my father, for Doris Appleby, for CHA and possibly for crime prevention everywhere.

Doris sat down and waited for comments.

Only one person made a comment. Me. I got up and said, "I don't think we should get all hot and bothered over a messed-up bedspread, candy wrappers and toothpaste, and I'm positive that somebody else in Camelot will agree with me."

Everybody, except the Tinker baby, turned and stared at me. Including my father. I hadn't yelled the loudest. I hadn't yelled the most often. I hadn't yelled the cleverest. I, Abby, had yelled the dumbest.

Chapter
9

The meeting went right on after I sat down. Lenny Tinker applauded, and that's all. After the meeting my father said, "I was glad to see you participating in the discussion. I'd like to hear more of your ideas."

"Right this very minute?"

"Oh no, it can wait. But let's talk some more soon."

"Why not," I said, even though I knew why not.

The next day at school I wondered if the person I really wanted to talk to would still be offering the back of her head as proof of her non-friendship. I saw Hutch handing out "The Family That Smokes Together Chokes Together" buttons, which her family had bought wholesale. She handed me a button. It was a hopeful start. Any refusal of hers to give me a health warning would have been the supreme sign that our friendship had permanently collapsed.

"Are you talking to me?" I asked.

"Yeah."

"Have you been thinking about what I said?"

"Yeah."

"So what do you think about it?"

"It makes sense."

Hutch was handing out buttons fast as she answered my questions. She was like one of those cooks flapping pancakes in a restaurant window. They're so good at what they're doing that they could be in a hypnotic trance and the pancakes would keep flapping. Hutch talked to me but she never stopped handing out the buttons.

"Hutch, do you really mean it?"

"Sure I really mean it. Why? Don't you think it makes sense?"

"Sure. That's why I said it. So now we're friends, right?"

"Right."

"Good. Now that we're friends again I'm not going to talk about being friends any more. Because it's all understood. Right?"

"Right."

Hutch handed out her last button. I pulled her into a corner. "Listen, Hutch, I've got something to tell you. The world is closing in on us, Hutch."

I liked using the word "us." It was such a *together* word.

"I don't get it," said Hutch.

Then I told Hutch about my father's interest in the Lancelot case and how he was digging into all kinds of angles. I told her what Doris Appleby had said at the meeting, and what I had said.

"It wasn't so smart but it wouldn't have been healthy to keep your thoughts inside you," Hutch said.

"You're not mad that I got involved?"

"No," said Hutch.

"Well, then aren't you concerned about my father? He's going to trace the candy and cakes next. Tell me that you bought them one by one, at a lot of different stores, please."

"How can I, when I bought them in one single glorious splurge at Racland's Variety Store? I cleaned out some of the racks. Mr. Racland said I had a sweet tooth."

"Then we're sunk, Hutch. We may as well admit what we did before they find out."

"Never," said Hutch.

Social Studies class started, and that put a stop to my conversation with Hutch.

Miss Forbes asked the kids if anyone did anything interesting during Memorial Day weekend. Everyone began to answer at once. Three kids had gone to Washington, D.C., two had gone upstate, five were sick, fifteen said they did nothing, and Monroe Firestone said to some kids near him, "I spent *my* time in King Arthur Country. Ah, that marvelous night at the Lancelot."

"Speak up, Monroe," said Miss Forbes.

Monroe said, "My Aunt Helen and Uncle Hy visited us, and I had to sleep on the living-room floor. I had a hard, hard weekend."

Miss Forbes managed a hard, hard smile.

After class, in the corridor, Monroe and his pal Evan were talking in very loud, everybody-ought-to-overhear-us voices. "It was beautiful. We got in, we got out, and nobody saw us. Did you read about us in the paper? No sign of forcible entry, it said. Of course not. We planned it perfectly."

A little crowd had gathered around Monroe and Evan. "C'mon, Monroe, you haven't got that kind of brain. You're all talk," someone said.

Monroe sort of sneered, and he and Evan walked away.

"Do you suppose they really were the ones?" someone asked.

"It seems like a Monroe kind of thing to do," somebody else said. "Anything to get attention. I mean *anything*."

Hutch was standing there, glaring. Lately Hutch had been glaring more and more, and I wondered where that fitted into her good-health plans. Now she pulled me into a corner. "Everybody is latching onto *my* idea and trying to get some credit for it," she said. "Either they say they did it, or they'll find out who did it. Everybody's got an angle. It's like a product that was pure and natural until people started adding artificial colors, flavors, preservatives, hardeners, softeners, mold inhibitors, alkalizers. . . ."

"Hutch," I interrupted. "Let's make it pure again. Let's tell Mr. Carstairs that we did it and we're sorry and ask him to call off the police. And then maybe my father will quit, too."

"But Carstairs is one of the polluters. He's giving it the artificial color and preservatives. That article in the paper. He got himself puffed up to twice his natural size."

"Hutch, just let's get finished with this whole business before it gets puffed up still more."

"No," said Hutch.

"O.K.," I said. "I give up."

That night a big sign was found in the master bedroom of the Lancelot. In huge black crayoned letters it said,

Hutch was waiting for me in front of school the next morning.

"Did you hear about the sign?" she asked me right away.

"Sure. All the kids are talking about it. You know something? I don't think we have to say anything to Mr. Carstairs after all. We just keep quiet and let everybody else talk."

"You mean brag," said Hutch. "The Lancelot was *my* idea and everybody's bragging about it."

"So what? You don't want anyone to know it was your idea."

Hutch didn't answer for about a minute. Then she said, "I probably never did anything in my life that was so terrific. And nobody even knows I did it except you and me."

"That's the terrific part," I said. "That last bit."

"You know what, Abby. If they knew I did it—*if*—they'd probably say, 'That Hutch Hutchins, when she scores, she *scores*. She's right up there with, well, with the great minds of history. Or at least the great minds of this school.'"

Hutch was quiet again. The bell rang and it was time to go to our first class.

After school Hutch and I walked home together. "I've been thinking," she said.

"About what?"

"About your idea to tell Mr. Carstairs everything. *Let's.* And he'll keep it a secret, of course, and our troubles will be over."

"Hutch," I said, "we don't have any troubles. Remember I told you this morning that the situation's changed."

"But I believe we should tell Mr. Carstairs," said Hutch. "I believe it down deep where I do all my believing."

"You didn't believe it the first time I asked you," I

said. "But, O.K. Then we'll really be finished with this whole thing forever and ever."

"Oh, sure," said Hutch. "Forever and ever."

Hutch had a look on her face that I had seen only once before. When she had been planning the Lancelot thing. She looked as if she were on the brink of something, ready to jump.

"Hutch," I said. "You scare me. And I don't know why."

We stopped in front of my house.

"Don't be scared, Abby," Hutch said. "Fright can be destructive to the body. Everything's going to be just fine."

Hutch walked on to her house. She was whistling. And she hardly ever whistled.

Chapter 11

After I ate a snack I went over to Hutch's house. She had just finished her snack, so she didn't offer me any. Which was O.K. with me.

I wanted to talk about Mr. Carstairs. Mr. Carstairs only comes to Camelot now and then. I think it's because he's a cautious man. Whenever I've seen him walking around, his head has been slightly bent as if ready to dodge anything that might be thrown at him by a dissatisfied resident. And he never comes on a regular basis or at a preannounced time. He must know that when you have a schedule that people can depend upon, like the changing of guards at a prison or the regular arrival of moneybags at a bank, it can encourage people who have violent intentions.

I said to Hutch, "Getting to talk with Mr. Carstairs won't be easy."

"Well, I see him sometimes coming and going at the Guinevere," Hutch said. "That's where his Camelot office is. But he spends most of his time at El Dorado and Shangri-la."

"What are they, and how do you know?"

"El Dorado and Shangri-la are two apartment houses that Mr. Carstairs is building in New Jersey. When I was getting ready for my Lancelot project, I learned all kinds of things I didn't have to learn. That's what happens when you're learning things you have to learn. You get an overflow."

"So how often is Mr. Carstairs around Camelot?"

"Not often. But I can tell when he's here. Unless I'm at school or somewhere like that. I can see the Guinevere from my bedroom window, and Mr. Carstairs has this really bright blue station wagon. So when I see the station wagon parked out there, I know Mr. Carstairs is around."

"But can you remember exactly how often you've seen it there?"

"Maybe once a week. Maybe less. That means we're going to have a tough time catching him."

"Hutch," I said, "maybe we should forget the whole thing."

"No," said Hutch.

"O.K., O.K. But you just watch for that bright blue station wagon, and the minute you see it, call me up and we'll go talk with Mr. Carstairs."

"I can do it myself if you want," said Hutch.

"No, we went to the Lancelot together, and we'll go to the Guinevere together."

"Oh," said Hutch.

I went home. I wanted to watch TV and just sort of go blank. Going blank is my favorite way to rest.

My father was busy typing, and Clyde was outside his door waiting for the typing to stop. When Clyde saw me he said, "I have to write a poem for my English homework, and one of the subjects I can choose from is 'Friendship' so I chose it and this is as far as I've gotten:

BETTY THE DOG

Betty is a cute dog.
She is black and white,
And when she sees another dog,
She starts an awful fight."

"That's nice," I said. "But what does it have to do with friendship?"

"Betty's my friend, that's what it's got to do with it.
Get it?"

My father stopped typing when he heard us talking.

"I'm trying to finish a chapter," he called. "How about
a little quiet?"

"I'm trying to finish a poem," said Clyde. "How about
a little help?"

My father came out of his room. He yawned. "Tell
you what," he said to Clyde and me, "I'll take a break

and do a little leg-stretching." He yawned again. "We'll take a walk, and we'll talk about the poem along the way. How about it?"

"Where to?" asked Clyde.

"Well, I was thinking of going to town to buy a candy bar," said my father.

"You were?" said Clyde.

My father looked at me. "You come, too, Abby. This will interest you. It's the Lancelot case. Remember the candy bars and cakes? I'm going to check the stores in town to see if anyone remembers selling them. Come with us."

Should I or shouldn't I? There are two stores in town that sell candy, Pierian's Luncheonette and Racland's Variety Store. Hutch spends time in both of them because they also sell *Health Is Wealth* magazine, which Hutch often stands around and reads. But Pierian's was safe. I knew that Racland's would be the scene of the disaster because of what Hutch had told me.

I decided to go. It would be like watching a horror show knowing that the prehistoric beast is—crash!— going to wreck the skyscraper with his foot whether I watch or not, so I watch.

Chapter
12

As we walked toward town, my father said, "Actually, Abby, I was waiting for you to come home so that you would have a chance to go with me. You seemed so involved in the Lancelot business the other night."

"I did?"

"Yes, but I don't agree with what you said. I think we *should* get all hot and bothered over this. When people fail to get hot and bothered over a seemingly small issue, eventually they might feel the same lassitude about larger issues."

"What's lassitude?" asked Clyde, who didn't know he was asking for both of us. Then he said, "Forget it. I've got another verse. You're supposed to be helping me with my poem, remember?

> *She romps in all the neighbors' yards,*
> *And does she love to play.*
> *She meets me on my way from school*
> *Almost every day.*

Do you like it so far?"

Clyde was looking at my father, but I answered.

"I love your poem," I said. And I did. I loved his poem because it had interrupted the Lancelot conversation.

"You love it? That's crazy," said Clyde. "I don't love it, so why should you? But I think it's O.K. Don't you, Dad? Don't you think it's O.K.?"

"Yes, it's certainly O.K. In fact, better than O.K.," said my father. "You really don't need my help."

"Yes I do," said Clyde.

We reached Pierian's Luncheonette just as Clyde finished reciting,

> *"She is a very nice little dog,*
> *But once in a while she's bad,*
> *And when she tipped the fishbowl,*
> *It made me very sad."*

Nobody at Pierian's remembered anyone buying a large amount of candy and cake at one time except for last Halloween. "Got to keep the witches, ghosts and monsters well fed, you know," said old Mr. Pierian.

My father smiled because he was supposed to, and Clyde and I smiled because we thought it was funny.

Racland's Variety Store was a few doors away. Clyde said,

> *"This little dog I'm writing about*
> *Doesn't belong to me,*
> *But what's the difference anyhow. . . ."*

The three of us walked into Racland's.

> *"I love her can't you see.*
> *The end."*

It seemed to me that Clyde's last two words were very appropriate for the occasion.

My father waited until Mr. Racland was through with a customer. Mr. Racland who owns the store is the father of Glenn. Laurie has not shared this information with our parents because of what might be called her activities at the store. I happen to know that for a long time she was the star customer of Racland's Variety Store. She had thought that Glenn might work there after school, or at least drop in to say hello to his father and his mother who also works there. Laurie had bought all her magazines, all her school supplies, all her greeting cards, everything that she possibly needed or might need that Racland's sold, before she finally found out that Glenn spent his afternoons at track practice.

"Yes?" said Mr. Racland.

"Could you possibly tell me whether any person or persons recently bought a large supply of candy bars and cakes from you at one time?" my father asked politely.

Mr. Racland seemed surprised by the question. But he rubbed his hand on his chin and wrinkled his forehead as if he were willing to work very hard to answer it.

"Oh, sure," he said suddenly. "But look, I didn't talk her into buying all that stuff. Never saw a girl with so much spending money. Almost every day she was in here for something. Friendly girl. Always hung around and talked to me when I wasn't busy. Lately she hasn't been coming in though. I guess her folks stopped her allowance."

"A girl?" said my father.

This didn't seem to be a good time for me to tell my father that Laurie was the girl whose allowance had regularly filled the cash register at Racland's.

Just then Mrs. Racland came in from a back room. Mr. Racland repeated my father's question and the answer he had given.

"Wait a minute, George," she said to her husband.

"That girl specialized in paper goods and supplies. Writing paper, notebooks, erasers, paper clips, greeting cards, gift wrapping, and magazines. She didn't buy very much that was fattening. I think she's one of those girls who watches what she eats. Probably got an eye on snagging a boyfriend."

It was clear that Mrs. Racland was the inventory expert for Racland's Variety Store. She remembered merchandise and she remembered people. She had a shopping-list mind, and Laurie was on her list on the same line with paper goods and supplies. Laurie was also on the same line with boyfriend, which Racland's Variety Store did not stock but which Laurie had hoped they could supply.

Mr. Racland spoke up. "My wife's right. That girl was big on paper, small on candy. But now I remember a girl coming in here about two weeks ago. She cleaned out the Chew City candy rack and all my little cakes. I tried to talk her out of the cakes because I knew they were stale. They came into the store stale. I was going to return them. But this kid was a determined kid."

"Who was she?" asked Mrs. Racland before my father could.

"I don't know her name," said Mr. Racland.

"What did she look like?" asked Mrs. Racland, again before my father could.

"The girl looked like—a girl. Sort of ordinary-looking. She comes in here now and then. I know her by sight. Anyway, she comes in with other ordinary-looking kids, like these kids here." He looked at my father. "Are these yours?"

"Yes," said my father.

"Sure," said Clyde. "Don't my sister and I look alike? Both ordinary."

I gave Clyde a dirty look on behalf of my father. My father said to Mr. Racland, "You don't know that girl's name? You don't know what she looked like?"

"I don't know her name," said Mr. Racland. "And I already told you what she looked like. Ordinary."

"But you'd know her if you saw her again?"

"I know all the kids when I see them again."

"But would you specifically know which one of the—uh—ordinary girls bought the candy and cakes?"

"I could *ask* which one did," said Mr. Racland, grinning like a football coach who had just thought of the play that would win the game. "But, of course," he said, "you'd have to tell me why you want to know. I mean, they're my *customers*. They may be kids, but the customer is always right, right?"

For some reason he looked at Clyde, and Clyde said, "You bet." Then Clyde said, "I want to go home."

My father thanked Mr. and Mrs. Racland and said he'd be back sometime. He bought Clyde and me each a candy bar, forgetting I wasn't supposed to eat it.

"That man and woman made me feel mixed-up," said Clyde as we walked up Main Street.

"I know what you mean," said my father. "I'll go back alone sometime. Maybe I'll jot down some questions that might prod Mr. Racland's memory. It seems now that the intruders might have been kids, and not adults. And possibly girls."

"Why don't you just give up?" said Clyde. "It's all so much trouble. I'm with Abby. I'm for no hot, no bother."

My father stopped walking. "Clyde, have you ever heard the legend of Excalibur?"

"Our house, the Excalibur? Is there already a legend about it?"

"Clyde," I said, "Dad means the *original* Excalibur. King Arthur's Excalibur."

"Oh sure, that one," said Clyde. "When you get used to the new one, sometimes you forget that the new one is just an idea copied from the old one. So what about the old one, Dad, the original?"

"Well, as you know, Excalibur was an enchanted sword. When Arthur first saw it, a hand was holding it up above water."

"You mean *that* Excalibur got flooded, too?"

My father laughed. Then he said, "On one side of the sword was written 'Take me,' and on the other side, 'Cast me away.' The story goes that the magician Merlin said to Arthur, 'Take thou and strike! The time to cast away is yet far off.' Well, Clyde, that's how I feel about pursuing this Lancelot affair. It's not yet time to quit."

As we reached home I was thinking how lucky King

Arthur had been to have something useful materialize. I didn't begrudge him his enchanted sword, but I thought I deserved a happy surprise, too. Like a bright blue station wagon parked in front of the Guinevere.

I now had the same hobby as Laurie. Waiting for the telephone to ring. Laurie was waiting for Glenn to call and I was waiting for Hutch. I found out that at the Memorial Day Parade Glenn had told Laurie he definitely would call her soon, and *she* was hopeful. I was getting discouraged. It had been two days since Hutch started to watch for Luther Carstairs's station wagon. When I saw her in school she said, "I do my homework at my desk by the window. I eat all my snacks by the window, and I've got a carpet full of sunflower and sesame seeds to prove it. When I'm not in my bedroom I set my mother's timer on the stove to go off every half hour to remind me to go look out the window. It's wrecked a couple of her meals, so I have to stop that. I'm giving it all I've got, Abby, but so far, no luck."

I knew that Hutch was trying hard. When she was committed to a project, she threw her whole unadulterated, unprocessed, natural self into it. But as it happened, I was the one who spotted Mr. Carstairs going into the Guinevere. After school on Friday, I took a walk over to Forest Road. Any kind of action, even useless action, seemed better than just waiting. My father was planning a return visit to Racland's Variety Store with a list of specific questions that couldn't be answered by the word ordinary. And Doris Appleby was planning a major attack to be launched against village officials for "allowing crime to prevail" in Camelot.

As I got near the Guinevere, a small green car pulled up in front of it. Luther Carstairs got out of the car and walked into the house. Just like that. I guess my mind works in strange ways sometimes because I rushed to Hutch's house to tell her the news that Luther Carstairs had changed cars, that instead of a bright blue station wagon, he now had a small green car. That was the big news that I was running to tell Hutch. By the time I got

to her house, my mind was back in good working order and I told Hutch the information that counted: Luther Carstairs was now in the Guinevere.

"But there's no blue station wagon there," said Hutch, who had rushed to her bedroom window immediately.

"He switched cars, Hutch. I saw him get out of that little green car."

"Switched cars, huh?" Hutch seemed angry, as if someone had played a trick on her. "Here you depend on something, and just like that it disappoints you."

Now Hutch was hung up on the changed cars.

"Hutch, people buy and sell cars every day. Anyway, it doesn't matter what Mr. Carstairs is driving. Let's just get over there before he leaves."

We ran to the Guinevere.

When we got there, Hutch opened the front door and

we walked in quietly. The inside of the Guinevere model home was decorated very much like the inside of the Lancelot model home. They certainly looked related.

There were just a few people walking around. "Weekdays are dull compared to weekends," Hutch explained. "Carstairs's office is in the den. Walk by the kitchen fast, or the salesman might see us and kick us out."

Hutch led the way. She knew exactly where to go. We stopped at the entrance to the den. Mr. Carstairs was bending over a desk. He heard us and looked up. His eyes, nose and mouth seemed entrenched in his face as if they had been at the same job for a very long time— doing guard duty for a fortress. But this fortress seemed tired, as if it had been charged one time too many and would crumble under the next assault. I felt sorry for him.

"Yes, girls?"

His voice wasn't friendly, and it wasn't unfriendly. It was a tired voice.

Hutch walked up to his desk. I followed. "We're residents of Camelot," said Hutch. "Abby here's got an Excalibur. I've got a Lancelot. Great houses."

Hutch was using two of her ideas which were, in my opinion, only remotely connected to good health. She was "establishing a relevant relationship" and "putting someone in a good mood."

But the tired fortress couldn't be reached that way.

"Do you want something, girls?"

I spoke up. "Yes, Mr. Carstairs, we came to tell you that we're the ones who entered the Lancelot model home last Sunday night. One of us spent the night there, the other, part of the night. But we're both equally to blame. We both messed up the place, but we didn't intend to. We really didn't. Really."

Mr. Carstairs's expression didn't change.

I went on. "I saw in the newspaper that $10.63 worth of damage was done. We're willing to repay that money."

"We are?" said Hutch.

My offer was a surprise to Hutch. It was also a surprise to me. I had just thought it up. But it was only fair.

Mr. Carstairs's expression still didn't change.

Hutch spoke. "I even spent the morning at the Lancelot. Until twenty past ten. I planned to leave before your salesmen came, but I overslept. When I heard the salesmen, I crawled under the bed. When the police came into the bedroom, the points of their shoes were about a foot from my nose. But they never looked under the bed. After the Lancelot opened for business, I walked out the way we walked in. My friend didn't tell you how we got in. Well, we walked in. Just natural. You know, I had this idea for a long time, spending the night at the Lancelot. It was all my idea, not my friend's. My friend came along because she's my friend."

Mr. Carstairs raised his hand in a kind of wave. "Thank you very much for telling me this, girls. Nice to have met you."

He picked up some papers and started to read them.

Hutch spoke again. "Did you hear us, Mr. Carstairs? We just *confessed*."

"And I thanked you," said Mr. Carstairs. "And I thank you again. And it was nice meeting you."

"I certainly thought you would want to hear who messed up your house," said Hutch.

"And I've heard," said Mr. Carstairs, putting down the papers. "I've heard from Joey Menderez, Jerome Goldberg, Chuck Schultz, Monroe Firestone, Evan somebody or other, and a couple of other boys, not to mention three girls. They all say they spent a night in the Lancelot. Jokers, that's what they are."

"But we really did it," said Hutch. "We're the real McCoy. Look, the newspaper didn't mention the brand of candy bars used, but I know. Most of them were Chew City. How do I know? Because I was there. Because I ate the candy. Bars and bars of Chew City."

Mr. Carstairs sat up very straight.

"*I* know who vandalized the Lancelot," he said. "Hoboes—homeless, sad, wandering tramps—found themselves a shelter for one night. But this country needs more well-built, economical, attractive houses such as the Camelot homes. If decent housing were available to everyone, people would not be tempted to occupy other people's property."

Oh boy! I looked at Hutch. Did she know what I knew? That Mr. Carstairs had just repeated his newspaper statement word for word, with the exception, I think, of the $10.63 sentence. Did Hutch also know what I now knew, that Mr. Carstairs didn't want to learn who was responsible for the Lancelot business. That he was glad it had happened. My father was right. For only $10.63 Mr. Carstairs had gotten himself a fortune's worth of good publicity.

Hutch knew. She was glaring at Mr. Carstairs. "Mr. Carstairs," she said. "We did it. *I* did it. I did it. I did it. I did it."

Mr. Carstairs looked straight at Hutch. "Well, what do you want me to do? Shout to the entire universe that you slept at the Lancelot?"

That was it! That was exactly what Hutch wanted Mr. Carstairs to do. Why hadn't I figured that out? Hutch had been too eager to speak to Mr. Carstairs. Sure. So he could tell everybody that *she* had done this fantastic Lancelot thing. He could even get it into the newspapers. Oh Hutch!

I spoke quickly. "No, we don't want anyone else to know, Mr. Carstairs. We want you to try to get the whole business quieted down. *Forgotten.* If you could just tell the police that you won't press charges, or maybe say that you found out who it was and they won't do it again."

"I get the idea," said Mr. Carstairs.

"I don't think you do," said Hutch. "My friend and I are fully prepared to accept the consequences—publicly —for what we did."

"Hutch, we are not!"

"*I* am!"

"Thank you both very much," said Mr. Carstairs. He picked up his papers, walked out of the house, and drove off in his little green car.

During the next few days, the topic of friendship was very big in my house. Clyde's teacher liked his friendship poem better than Clyde did. Which confused Clyde.

"It isn't as good as she says it is," said Clyde.

"Your poem shows a feeling of true friendship," said my mother, who liked the poem even better than the teacher did. "Finish your meat, Clyde."

I myself was no longer a believer in true friendship. I had stopped speaking to Hutch. I was disgusted with her.

And her scheme had failed. When my father went to the police station again, he was told that the case was somewhere between inactive and dead. The police said that Mr. Carstairs did not want to press charges against anybody, and since nothing was stolen, there was, in fact, no real case. I personally think that Mr. Carstairs isn't a bad guy at all, and I also think that the future is bright for Camelot. Especially when it doesn't rain.

My father didn't give up right away, though. He made the return visit to Racland's. He came back mumbling, "Ordinary, ordinary. Some people have a restricted vocabulary."

Fortunately, Laurie didn't know that my father was referring to Glenn's father. Fortunately, too, my father didn't know that he was referring to Glenn's father. The Raclands themselves have not, as yet, been discussed at our supper table. But that will change soon. On Wednesday, at exactly 6:15 P.M.—in the middle of supper, of course—Glenn called Laurie for a date. It won't be long before everybody knows who everybody else is, and my father will have to get used to the idea of Laurie being friendly with Ordinary's son, just as Glenn's mother will have to get used to Glenn being friendly with the Star Purchaser of Paper Goods and Supplies. But I guess it will all work out.

Also on Wednesday, Clyde brought home a friend, a

person, Scott Hopper, soon to be renamed "Fingers" by our family. Scott is a quiet boy who walked through our house handling everything he could lay his hands on, including our new white curtains. He dented a lampshade, scratched our piano, and left prints—finger *and* foot—in every room. Still, I think it's good for Clyde to branch out from dogs.

Yesterday Hutch tried to make up with me. She came up to me at school and talked to the back of my neck. "Abby, I'm sorry I did what I did. I never wanted marks for the Lancelot thing. But it got so big and so great. And suddenly I needed it a lot, the credit, I mean. I needed it more than anything. Get it?"

"Maybe."

"I don't," said Hutch. "I just don't."

Hutch was on my mind all day at school, and I knew I wanted to be friends again. I looked for her after my last class, but I didn't see her, so I walked over to her house.

I rang the back doorbell, but it was Mrs. Hutchins who answered it, so I knew immediately that Hutch

wasn't home. She said that Hutch would be home in an
hour. I was about to walk away, but I didn't. I stared at
Mrs. Hutchins. I was feeling bold. *Me*, Abby.

"Mrs. Hutchins," I said, "Hutch is hung up on marks.
She doesn't want to want them but she wants them.
That's maybe because you tell her whether every little
thing she does is good or bad, or even medium. Mrs.
Hutchins, you're squashing Hutch."

Mrs. Hutchins smiled in her very special unconnected

kind of way and said, "You're a funny little girl, Abby. When you grow up, I imagine you'll try to be a psychologist. Hutch might become one, too. She's good at analyzing. Very Good."

Then Mrs. Hutchins offered me a piece of fruit.

I said, "No, I'm terrible at eating," which I knew was rude, and I left.

An hour later, Hutch came over. She said, "Know what my mother asked me just now? Here's a direct quote: 'Am I squashing you? Tell me, am I squashing you?' "

"I asked her where she got an idea like that, and she said she got it from you. She said that tonight she and my father and I are going to have a squash talk."

"Good," I said. "I think."

Hutch doesn't like big make-up scenes, so that's all I said. By the way, I'm glad that we made up for the right reason, because otherwise we would have had to make up for the wrong reason. Remember, I have this belief that people who are in trouble together can't afford to be enemies. It isn't exactly that we're in trouble, but there has been a new development that Hutch hasn't heard about yet. Last night the Lancelot was robbed. The real thing. My father told me. Fixtures and furniture were taken. Among the items stolen were several chairs, which is very hard to believe, but robbers don't have time to try out merchandise before they steal it.

According to my father, the police have a theory that this robbery might have been carried out by the same person or persons who vandalized the Lancelot on Memorial Day weekend. The police are now, at this moment, searching the premises very thoroughly.

This last bit of information has inspired me to remember where my missing socks are. I dropped them into the clothes hamper in the bathroom at the Lancelot, just as I would have done at home. I was a real-life Queenie, so to speak, powdering my nose at the scene of the crime. This wouldn't bother me too much, except that I also remember that each sock has a name tape sewn into it, with my name printed in the laboratory-tested, fade-proof, bright red script that I had personally chosen before I went away to camp last summer.

But I plan to keep calm and live each day at a time, which is another good-health recommendation of Hutch's.